dick bruna

miffy and the new baby

SIMON AND SCI
London   New Y

Mummy and Daddy Bunny

have some special news to tell.

And one spring day they think it's time

that Miffy knows as well.

There's going to be a baby bunny

Miffy hears them say.

She hops about with happiness

and shouts a loud hurray!

I'll make a picture now, she thinks,

for baby, as a treat,

with little chicks to look at,

all yellow, small and sweet.

In Miffy's finished picture

there are eight cute chicks in all.

Miffy's Daddy makes a frame

and hangs it on the wall.

Then Mummy brings a ball of wool.

Would Miffy like that too?

Oh yes, says Miffy, good idea,

I'll make a mouse in blue.

So Miffy makes a woolly mouse.

How busy she has been!

Her woolly mouse looks really good,

the best we've ever seen.

Then Mummy Bunny pats her tummy

with her hands one day,

and says, I think our baby

is nearly on its way.

And sure enough, right after that

the time goes by so fast.

Soon Miffy's Daddy comes to say

– the baby's here at last!

Baby Bunny's tucked in bed,

all dreamy, sweet and dozy.

Mummy Bunny looks so pleased.

She'll keep her baby cosy.

Miffy stands beside the bed.

She hadn't known at all

that it would be so tiny,

so very cute and small.

And Miffy is allowed to hold

the baby on her knee.

It makes her feel so grown-up

and proud as she can be.

When Miffy goes to school next day

what's this she has to take?

To share with all her special friends,

a 'Welcome Baby' cake!

Original title: kleine pluis
Original text Dick Bruna © copyright Mercis Publishing bv, 2003
Illustrations Dick Bruna © copyright Mercis bv, 2003
This edition published in Great Britain in 2014 by Simon and Schuster UK Limited
1st Floor, 222 Gray's Inn Road, London WC1X 8HB, A CBS Company
Publication licensed by Mercis Publishing bv, Amsterdam
English re-translation by Tony Mitton © copyright 2014, based on the
original English translation of Patricia Crampton © copyright 2002
ISBN 978 1 4711 2212 5
Printed and bound by Sachsendruck Plauen GmbH, Germany
A CIP catalogue record for this book is available from the British Library upon request
10 9 8 7 6 5 4 3 2 1

www.simonandschuster.co.uk

MIX
From responsible
sources
FSC® C021195
www.fsc.org